Baby Bill and
Little Lil's
house

For Ann-Janine

KINGFISHER
Larousse Kingfisher Chambers Inc.
95 Madison Avenue
New York, New York 10016

First published in 1999
2 4 6 8 10 9 7 5 3 1
1TR/0599/TWP/RPR(RPR)/170NMA

LIBRARY OF CONGRESS CATALOGING-IN-PUBLICATION DATA
Heap, Sue.
Baby Bill and Little Lil / written and illustrated by Sue Heap.
—1st ed.
p.   cm.
Summary: In search of a pet fishy, Little Lil and Baby Bill rush
down a hill, accompanied by a menagerie of animals, and almost come
to an unhappy end.
[1. Animals Fiction. 2. Fishes Fiction.]   I. Title.
PZ7.H34465Bab   1999
[E]—dc21   99-13059   CIP

ISBN 0-7534-5196-4
Printed in Singapore

Baby Bill and Little Lil

Sue Heap

KING*f*ISHER

NEW YORK

In a house at the top of the hill,
lived Baby Bill and Little Lil.
Baby Bill wanted a pet.
He wanted a pet fishy.
So Little Lil said, "Let's go fishing."

"Hello!" said Clive Cat.
"Where are you heading?"
"To catch a pet fishy," said Little Lil.
"Yummy," Clive Cat meowed.
"I love fishing."

"YOO-HOO!" waved Dilly Dog.
"Can I play, too?"
"Please do," said Little Lil.
So Dilly Dog followed Clive Cat,
Little Lil, and Baby Bill down the hill.

"BAA!" called Sam, Sue, and Sid Sheep.
"Don't leave us, ple-ee-ase."
So Sam, Sue, and Sid Sheep followed
Dilly Dog, Clive Cat, Little Lil, and Baby Bill
all going faster down the hill.

Up above were Bird and Bee.
"Do you think they're going to a party?"
said Bee. "Let's follow and see."

"Is the fishy very far?" asked Baby Bill.
"Not so far now," said Little Lil.
"Faster!" shouted Baby Bill.
So Sam, Sue, and Sid Sheep, Dilly Dog, and
Clive Cat followed Little Lil and Baby Bill
faster and faster down the hill.

Baby Bill began to run.
He dropped his pail.
"Watch out!" shouted Bird.

But it was too late . . . .

OOSH!

They tumbled in the air.

BUMP! They landed on the sand.
"Phew!" said Little Lil. "Are we all here?"
"Waah," wailed Baby Bill.
"I've lost my pail!"

Clive Cat saw it, shining in the evening sun.

But a great big wave came
and took Baby Bill's pail away.

"Waah, waah!" cried Baby Bill.
"It's getting dark," bleated
Sam, Sue, and Sid Sheep.
"Let's go home," said Little Lil.

Waah!
Waah!

So Sam, Sue, and Sid Sheep,
Dilly Dog, and Clive Cat
followed Little Lil and Baby Bill
slowly, slowly up the hill.
"Good night, everyone," called Bird and Bee.

"Waah, I want my pail,"
whimpered Baby Bill.
"Waah, I want my fishy."
"Don't waah, Baby Bill," said Little Lil.
"Start wishing—we'll wait
for the light of the moon."

Softly, softly, Little Lil and Baby Bill
tiptoed back to the bottom of the hill....

In came the waves; in came the pail.

In the pail was a little fishy.
"My pet fishy!" said Baby Bill.
"Thank you, Moon," said Little Lil.
And Baby Bill and Little Lil danced hand
in hand by the light of the lovely old moon.

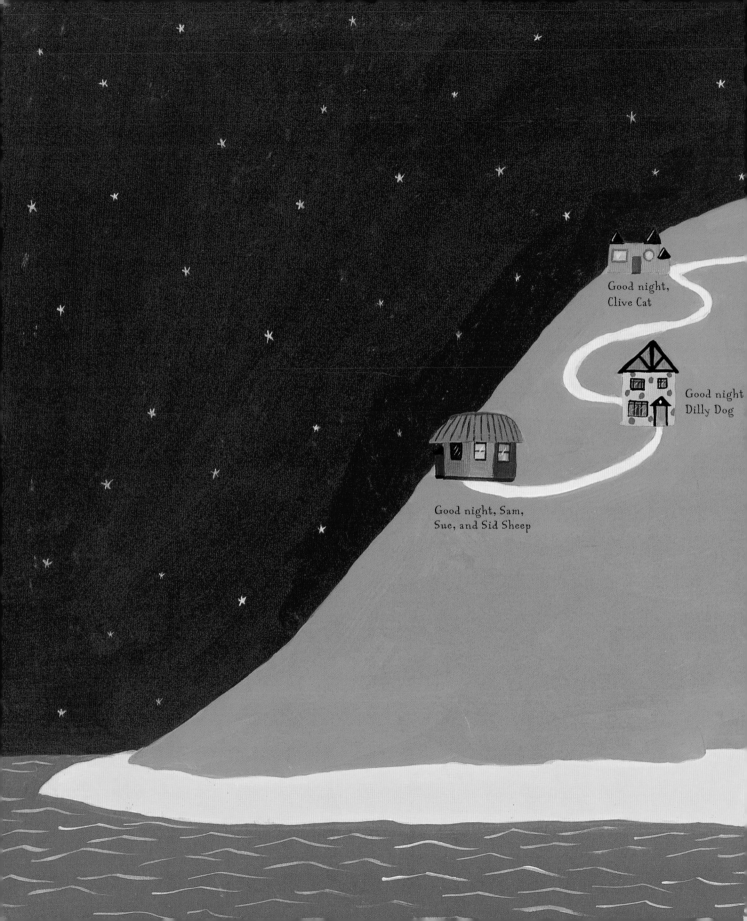

Good night,
Clive Cat

Good night
Dilly Dog

Good night, Sam,
Sue, and Sid Sheep